To my dear friend, Harsham,
with love from
Julie Florence 24.2.98

THE NEW RECTOR

Julie Florence

MINERVA PRESS
LONDON
MONTREUX LOS ANGELES SYDNEY

THE NEW RECTOR
Copyright © Julie Florence 1998

All Rights Reserved

No part of this book may be reproduced in any form,
by photocopying or by any electronic or mechanical means,
including information storage or retrieval systems,
without permission in writing from both the copyright owner
and the publisher of this book.

ISBN 1 86106 860 3

First Published 1998 by
MINERVA PRESS
195 Knightsbridge
London SW7 1RE

Printed in Great Britain for Minerva Press

THE NEW RECTOR

Chapter One

Jane was digging the vegetable patch in the large Rectory garden. She stopped to watch a robin pulling at a worm just a few feet away.

'Oh, how beautiful you are,' she whispered. She watched the robin for a full minute until it flew off into a nearby lilac bush, replete.

I must get this vegetable patch dug before tonight, she thought. Then I can sow the seeds tomorrow. It certainly is very hard work.

Jane continued digging, whistling a little ditty. She had just another couple of rows to dig then she could stop for the day. The sun was very warm and she felt extremely tired but she carried on regardless.

The back garden was neatly set out with rosebushes bordering a long path to an old summerhouse. Broom and lavender bushes were dotted here and there and alpine plants and heathers were growing in profusion around the large expanse of lawn. At the end of the garden, near the high stone wall, conifers grew in beautiful shades of blue, green and gold.

A car drove along the narrow, winding road, flanked on either side with hawthorn bushes, entered the quiet village and pulled up outside the church. The occupant sat for a while in deep thought looking at the church then got out and walked up the cobbled pathway to the south door. A notice board read 'Welcome to St Joseph's Parish Church'. He was in luck; the church was open. Just inside there was a holy water stoup in which he dipped a finger and crossed himself. The church smelled of incense; he nodded his head and smiled. Everything looked well-kept and polished and flowers adorned every nook and cranny. 'Must have had a flower festival recently,' he murmured to himself. There were twelve rows of pews on either side of the nave aisle and the same in both north and south aisles. There were two side altars and the high altar looked very impressive with a green and gold brocade frontal. The organ was situated on the south side of the chancel; the pipes painted gold; a full fan-shaped pedal board and several good stops. The choir-stalls were long and the seats padded. 'They're probably used to long sermons!' he chuckled. He knelt down at the altar rail and prayed. He felt at peace here; there was a strong atmosphere and he liked it. He left the church and as he walked back to the car the church clock struck three fifteen. He continued his journey along the same road and looking to either side of him as he drove slowly saw a sign outside a large house marked 'The Rectory'.

'So this is the Rectory,' said the young man to himself. 'What a rambling old house! Come on, Brandy, we may as well have a look round now we're here.'

The man and a golden Labrador got out of the car and entered the sweeping driveway. The man noted the well-kept garden containing bright spring flowers and neatly trimmed conifers. A lone pear-tree stood to the left of the house from which a song thrush sang. A squirrel scrambled up a nearby oak-tree and Brandy bounded after it. The man smiled as he continued his saunter to the back of the house where he saw a young girl digging. She was wearing a plain brown dress and gardening boots; her dark brown, waist-length hair was tied back with a yellow ribbon. He watched her for some time, then Brandy came and lay at his feet.

'Catch your squirrel, Brandy?'

The dog pricked up his ears at the sound of his name and gave a bark. Jane, startled at the sudden noise, looked up from her hard labour and saw a handsome young man dressed in a black suit and clerical collar, smiling at her.

'Hello, there!' said the priest.

'Hello, Father,' she said, surprised. 'You did make me jump!'

'I'm sorry,' he said, still smiling and striding along the path to join her. 'I've come to look at the Rectory; rather old, isn't it?'

'Yes, it is, but there is some lovely oak panelling in most of the rooms, and the central stairway is well worth seeing,' said Jane. Then she enquired, 'Are you thinking of coming here?'

'Well, the thought had crossed my mind, but I have been looking at other parishes in the area,' he said.

'Oh, I see,' said Jane.

As the priest continued to look at her Jane became embarrassed and felt her face redden. She looked away. She had never seen such a handsome young man before, such dark brown eyes and jet-black hair, and he must be all of six feet tall.

'I'm Father Stephen James,' he said. 'May I ask your name?'

'I'm Jane West. I live at the orphanage at the top of the hill; you may have seen it as you came into the village.'

'Oh, yes, I remember now; rather a dark and gloomy looking place.'

'Yes, I'm afraid so,' replied Jane, 'we had a fire not long ago.'

'Nothing serious, I hope?' said Father Stephen.

'No, it was only a small fire,' said Jane. 'The cook left some vegetables boiling merrily away and forgot about them. The kitchen was smelling of smoke for quite some days afterwards.'

Then Father Stephen asked, suddenly changing the subject, 'How old are you, Jane?'

'I'm eighteen, Father,' she replied, rather surprised at his asking her such a personal question. 'I'm the eldest at the orphanage, although Matron still treats me as one of the younger ones,' she said, with a rueful smile.

'And how long have you been at the orphanage?' he asked.

'I've been there since I was two years old,' she replied. Her eyes started to fill with tears as she went on to tell him about the car accident which killed both her parents and how soon afterwards her maternal grandmother had died of cancer. Her paternal grandparents had emigrated to Australia some years before and were so engrossed in their business that they had no time for her; consequently she went to the orphanage and had been there ever since.

She ended by saying, 'I can't remember a home of my own. I was in the back seat of the car and was saved by the safety belt on the child's seat, but I was told years later that I had had concussion and that may be the reason why I can't remember what happened before the accident.'

Father Stephen put a hand on her shoulder and said, 'I'm sure one day you will have your own home, Jane, if that's what you really want.'

'Oh, yes it is,' she said with fervour.

'Then you must continue to pray, Jane,' he said. 'Never give up.'

Father Stephen glanced around the garden and liked what he saw. It had been well tended and pleasantly set out. A garden seat stood in a shady corner surrounded by heather. He asked, 'Have you done all this digging, Jane?'

'Yes, Father,' she said putting a hand up to her hair to brush away a stray strand. As she did so Father Stephen noticed how blistered the hand was.

'How long have you been working here today?' There was a sharp tone in his voice.

'Since nine o'clock this morning, Father,' Jane replied.

'Since when?' he erupted. 'It's three thirty now!'

Jane was shocked at the sudden change of temper and said, stammering, 'I... I'm afraid I had... no idea it was... so late.'

Father Stephen took the spade from her and thrust it into the newly dug soil. He took her hands in his and turned them palm upwards. Jane looked up at him like a frightened creature. His eyes met hers and he said gently, 'I think you've done quite enough for one day. I've a first aid kit in the car; I'll see to your hands.'

Jane looked down at her hands and saw what a poor state they were in, and it was then she felt them throbbing with pain.

'We may as well go through the Rectory, it is open,' she said. 'I've been given a key so that I can come and keep the place clean, and if necessary put on the central heating if it gets really cold.'

'I'd like to have a look around,' he enthused, 'but we must see to your hands first. Come on, Brandy, you may as well come too,' he said, patting the dog's head. Brandy barked. They moved towards the kitchen door.

'He's a lovely dog,' said Jane. 'How long have you had him?'

'About three years now,' he said. 'He's a good guard dog!'

'I'm sure he is!' said Jane.

The kitchen was quite large, with modern amenities, and spotlessly clean. The quarry tiled floor shone and the wooden wall cabinets smelled of polish.

'I'll show you through to the hall and the front door,' said Jane. 'The hall is very large, and I understand previous incumbents used to entertain there, but only in the summer as there is no form of heating.'

'It must be pretty cold in winter,' said Father Stephen, ruefully.

'There is a cupboard under the stairs which houses four convector heaters, so if it is extremely cold they can be used.'

'It would be warmer with a fitted carpet,' said Father Stephen, 'but the floor is beautifully polished and it would be a pity to cover it all. Have you polished this, Jane?'

'Yes, I love coming here and looking after things, and when I get a house of my own I hope it's like this,' she said ecstatically.

They reached the beautiful oak front door and Jane turned the key. The door opened without a creak.

'Well oiled!' said Father Stephen, and laughed.

Jane smiled and Father Stephen ran down the steps to his car with Brandy hot on his heels.

Jane watched. He's so full of energy! she thought. Not at all like Father Joshua, although he was seventy!

Father Stephen came back carrying a small first aid box and they went back into the kitchen and sat at the table. He treated Jane swiftly and then closed the box.

'There, Jane,' he said, 'that should help things along nicely.'

'Thank you very much, Father, I'm very grateful to you,' she said shyly. 'You seem to know all about first aid!'

'My mother was a nurse,' said Father Stephen. 'She died last year.'

'Oh, I'm so sorry,' said Jane.

'She taught me all I needed to know about first aid at an early age. Well,' he said, changing the subject abruptly, 'are you going to show me the rest of the house?'

'I'd love to,' said Jane. 'I'll show you the study first, it's at the front of the house next to the kitchen.'

Off they went with Brandy padding along after them, sniffing every nook and cranny. The study was extraordinarily large with a bay window. The previous incumbent had left a large desk and chair; the latter with its back to the window. A large fireplace stood at the left of the desk and the room was carpeted throughout.

'It's very light in here,' commented Father Stephen. 'But of course there are no curtains.'

'Father Joshua took those with him,' said Jane. 'They were about the only curtains which fitted his new home. He left many things because he just didn't have room for them. Shall I show you the rooms upstairs now?'

'Yes, please do,' said Father Stephen.

As they crossed the hall Jane pointed to another door which she said led into the lounge and said she would show him the room later. They climbed the wide staircase to a landing, and facing the stairs was the first door. 'This is one of the bedrooms,' she said, opening the door. It was bare, but for curtains at the leaded windows and rugs on the floor. 'The room next to this is the bathroom.'

They went in and Father Stephen was surprised at seeing a shower unit. 'All mod cons!' he said, smiling broadly, and laughed.

'Oh, yes,' said Jane. 'A lot of work was done on the house about two years ago, including rewiring and having gas central heating. They just didn't bother with the hall!'

'Mm,' said Father Stephen. 'I don't like the colour of the walls in here. I shouldn't want a lot of decorating to do if I came.'

'Well, I'm sure Mr Scott, the church-warden could help you out there, he's a professional painter and decorator – and Mr Belton, the PCC treasurer, is a plumber,' said Jane.

'Very useful people to have around!' enthused Father Stephen. 'What's across the corridor?' he said, pointing to the opposite door.

'That's the master bedroom,' said Jane, 'and would you believe it has an old four-poster bed in it!'

'Indeed,' said Father Stephen, raising his eyebrows.

He opened the door and Brandy rushed past them and ran under the bed.

'He's having a more thorough look around!'

They both laughed and Brandy barked.

The four-poster bed stood facing the door. The trimmings were of crimson brocade, slightly faded with the passing years, but still in reasonable condition. Rugs covered most of the floor, and again the room was spotlessly clean. Father Stephen walked over to the bed and sat on it.

'Quite firm,' he said, and grinned.

'The mattress sags in the middle, though,' said Jane.

'And how would you know that, young lady?' teased Father Stephen.

Jane blushed and said, 'One evening last winter I was here cleaning and there was a huge snowstorm with six feet high drifts, it went on for hours. I rang Matron and she suggested I stay here the night, so I slept in this bed.'

'You weren't frightened being here on your own?' said Father Stephen.

'No, not really,' said Jane.

They went out of the room and Jane showed Father Stephen a stairway at the end of the corridor which led to the attic. 'There is nothing up there as far as I know. Some of the doors are locked and I don't know who would hold the keys; probably the church-wardens.'

'We may as well go and look at the lounge now,' said Father Stephen. 'I'm afraid I have to be back in London by 7 p.m. Come on, Brandy, there's nothing else for you to see up here!'

Brandy raced downstairs and ran round the hall and sniffed at the front door.

'He seems to like it here,' said Jane, timidly, hoping that Father Stephen would become their parish priest. She patted his head and he wagged his tail. They went into the lounge which was on the other side of the hall to the study and looked almost an exact replica, apart from there being no desk. The wallpaper was a mid green colour, quite pleasing to the eye, with gold coloured curtains. There was no furniture in the room.

'It is very pleasant,' said Father Stephen quietly. 'There seems to be a warmth about the place, despite the cold hall!' They both laughed and Father Stephen said, 'Well, Jane, thank you very much for showing me around, I do hope your hands get better quickly.' He put out his hand to shake Jane's and he held it very gently. 'Thank you, Jane,' he said again, and smiled.

'I'm glad you had the opportunity to look round,' said Jane. 'You have seen the church?'

'Yes, I called in there on my way here,' he said. Very well kept! I do like to see plenty of flowers.'

'Yes,' said Jane, 'we had a flower festival last weekend and raised £2000.'

'That is excellent in such a small community,' said Father Stephen, surprised.

'We all worked very hard, Father.'

'And were well rewarded,' he said. 'God bless you, Jane, and goodbye.'

'Thank you, Father, goodbye.'

Jane opened the wide front door for him and patted Brandy's head again as they went down the steps to the car.

'Have a safe journey,' Jane called.

'Thank you, Jane. I may see you again sometime.'

Jane smiled and waved. 'I do hope so,' she whispered to herself.

Chapter Two

The weeks went by and nothing was heard about a new incumbent. Jane never told anyone about meeting Father Stephen. She wanted to keep it a secret, something only she would know about. She went to the Rectory as often as she could to tend the garden and to clean the rooms. The seeds she had planted were growing nicely now and she was quite proud of them.

'Such a pity if they go to waste,' she sighed one day when she was hoeing around the plants. 'Never mind, they'll be useful at the Harvest Festival.'

The next day was Sunday, and like all Sundays, Jane and the other children at the orphanage attended Sung Mass at 10.30 a.m. The Rural Dean was visiting them today. Jane liked him, he was quite a jovial man and made his sermons interesting with little stories. The Gradual hymn finished and the Gospel was read amidst clouds of incense. The Rural Dean climbed the pulpit steps and read out two sets of banns and the notices for the week, which was the custom at St Joseph's at that stage of the service.

'And now the moment you've all been waiting for,' said the Rural Dean with rapture. There were a few groans from the choir stalls. The Rural Dean turned to face the choir and leaned over the pulpit. 'And it ain't me sermon!' he said, grinning at a red-faced choirboy.

The church filled with titters and guffaws then fell silent. 'I've come to tell you that you have a new incumbent,' he said. The congregation gasped; they were all ears now and Jane held her breath. They had been nearly two years without an incumbent and now the time had come for them to have one.

'O, please God, let it be Father Stephen,' she prayed.

'He's a young man, a celibate, and he's been a curate at a church in London, so this will be his first parish. He's a workaholic and expects others to work, so look after him. His name is Father Stephen James. Oh, and he absolutely adores bread-and-butter pudding!' The congregation laughed till the rafters proverbially shook. The Rural Dean began his short sermon. 'May the words of my mouth...' were all the words Jane heard. It seemed as though she was in a trance, she felt so happy. The sermon ended and the Offertory hymn was announced. Jane sang but was not taking in the words. When she went into the chancel with the other communicants she seemed like an automaton. When she knelt down to receive communion she prayed very hard that Father Stephen would be happy with them and that everyone would make him welcome. And then a cold shiver went down her spine. Perhaps he won't need anyone to do the cleaning or tend the garden, she thought. She felt sick. She had so loved keeping the Rectory clean and the garden neat. She went back to the orphanage with a heavy heart.

The date for the induction was given as 20th June at 7 p.m. The usual flower ladies made a splendid job of the summer garden flowers in church; it looked quite like a flower festival, and the Mother's Union prepared for a slap-up bun-fight afterwards!

Jane helped where she could. She just wanted to do something for him. Matron was busy making sure the children were looking their best, if that were at all possible!

'My collar's too tight,' groaned William.

'Where's my left shoe?' shouted Susan.

'Matron, my dress has a tear in it!' cried Helen.

'You'll have to wear another one, dear,' said Matron, getting quite exasperated. 'I haven't time to mend it now.'

The emergencies over, Matron shuffled the children into a reasonably orderly line with about twenty minutes to spare to get them to the church. Jane walked at the rear to see none of the children went missing. She felt very nervous. Would Father Stephen even remember her?

The children filed into church and sat about halfway down the nave. The church was getting very full. Many people had come from Father Stephen's previous parish and, as Jane looked about her, she saw that most of the villagers were there, all in their Sunday best!

The service started with the hymn 'The Church's One Foundation', while the crucifer, followed by the small choir, emerged from the vestry up the north aisle and down the nave. Jane's heart was beating rapidly as the choir passed her. Soon she would see Father Stephen. There he was! She saw the back of his head as he passed her. He had a lovely tenor voice.

After the service everyone trooped over to the church hall for a feast. A few welcoming words were said and then Jane saw Father Stephen moving through the throng, chatting with everyone. Jane stood near the door with a plate of food in one hand and a drink in the other, watching him. She still felt very nervous and couldn't eat much and just kept smiling at the people moving past her but keeping a watchful eye on him. He was getting nearer now, talking to Mr Belton, the treasurer. Jane's attention was distracted by one of the orphans running past her out of the door with another child in hot pursuit.

'Oh, Jane,' said Matron, 'did you see where William and Simon went?'

'Yes, they've gone outside,' was Jane's reply.

'Would you go and find them, dear, I must go and round the others up and take them back, they're getting too excited,' she said, rather tired.

'Oh, I... yes, of course,' stammered Jane, 'I'll go right away.'

Jane was heartbroken. She wanted to speak to Father Stephen and now she had to go after those naughty boys and then leave the party early. She put her plate and glass down on the nearest table and went looking for them. She was almost in tears when she found them and gave them a good telling-off. When she got back to the church hall the boys ran in ahead of her and found Matron and the other children gathered together in one corner. She was just going to get her coat when she heard her name.

'Jane!'

She looked round and standing behind her was Father Stephen.

'I've been looking for you, Jane,' he said, 'you disappeared!'

'I had to go and bring back two of the children who had run off,' she said shyly. 'How are you?'

'I'm very well, Jane,' he said quietly, 'how are you?'

'I'm so pleased you've come here,' she blurted out. 'I mean... I'm glad it's you,' she stammered, reddening.

'I'm very pleased to be here, Jane,' he said. 'I was looking for you because I wanted to ask you if you'll be willing to be my housekeeper. It is a very large house, as you know,' he said smiling, 'and I quite simply need someone to help me. You've done marvels with the polishing! Will you be my housekeeper, Jane?' he said. And for the first time there seemed to be a nervousness about him. He looked at her intently and she replied:

'I should love to be your housekeeper, Father. I still have a key which I was going to give you back.'

'There's no need, you must keep it. Come to the Rectory tomorrow morning, if you can, and we'll arrange something. Could you be there by about ten o'clock?'

'Yes, of course.'

'Then I'll see you tomorrow, Jane,' he said offering her his hand.

'See you tomorrow, Father,' she replied, taking his hand. Did she detect a slight squeeze? And then he turned away, to converse with some members of the choir and the organist.

Jane and Matron took the children back to the orphanage and prepared them for bed. What a hard task they had that night! The children were so excited, none of them wanted to go to bed. They just talked and talked about the lovely food they had eaten, and of course, the inevitable – a number of them were sick through eating too much! Jane finally crawled into bed at about twelve thirty, very tired but very happy – she would be seeing Father Stephen tomorrow and would be able to show him what she had done in the garden.

The following day Jane woke early, despite being very tired the previous night, and before she could get out of bed Matron knocked gently on her door.

'Come in,' said Jane.

'Oh, Jane,' said Matron. 'I've been up half the night with Peter and Susan, they've been sick most of the time, would you mind having a look at them now, I must go into the village for some provisions.'

'Yes, of course,' said Jane, hoping against hope she would be back before she was due to go to the Rectory; but then, that was selfish of her, and if the children needed her then she must stay. She had yet to mention to Matron about Father Stephen offering her the post of housekeeper.

'By the way,' said Matron, 'I'll do my best to get back before your visit to the Rectory.' Jane stared at her, her face reddening. 'Father Stephen told me last night that he intended asking you if you would become his housekeeper, and I told him it was an excellent idea, although I do hope you will come and help me here sometimes,' she said rather hopefully.

'Oh, Matron, of course I will,' said Jane. 'I was going to have a word with you about it as soon as I could. I'm so glad you don't mind. I do love being here, it's like home.'

'Well,' said Matron, 'this is your home for as long as you need it, Jane.'

'Thank you, I'm very happy here, really I am.'

'Now that's sorted out,' said Matron with tears filling her eyes, 'I'll go and see what I can get from the butcher. Peter and Susan should be asleep now, but if you'll just look in on them, I'd be grateful,' and with that she gently shut the door.

Jane duly went to see Peter and Susan, and as Matron said, they were fast asleep. She made herself a cooked breakfast and tidied the lounge which was full of toys. The other children were at school and the orphanage seemed so peaceful. She opened a lounge window which looked across the village and in the distance she could see the beautiful heather on the heath. She loved to walk on the heath – its wide open space – it was so refreshing. She could also see the Rectory chimney-pots and the rear bedroom windows and she wondered what he would be doing now. Would he be writing his sermon or choosing prayers for the intercessions; answering the telephone to someone in need or wanting to arrange a wedding or funeral. Little did she know at that moment in time he was trying to replace a washer on a very old, obstinate tap in the bathroom sink! Such incidents do happen to occur occasionally even to priests!

'I'm back, Jane!' came Matron's breezy call with a slam of the front door. Jane met her in the hall and offered to carry some of the shopping bags into the kitchen.

'No, it's all right, Jane, you run along now, you mustn't keep the Rector waiting on your first morning, I can manage.' With that Jane ran to her room and looked frantically in her wardrobe for a coat. They all looked so drab! She chose a pale blue cardigan instead, combed her hair quickly and rushed down the stairs. The telephone rang.

'Oh, no!' exclaimed Jane. But Matron shooed her out of the front door and answered it herself.

'It's lovely to be outside in the fresh air!' said Jane under her breath. 'Good morning, Mr Peters!' she shouted, across the road to an old man on a rickety bicycle.

'And a lovely morning it is too, Jane!' he answered. 'An' where might you be off to in such a hurry?' he said, getting off his bicycle and pushing it across the road to her.

'I'm going to the Rectory, Mr Peters; the new Rector wants me to be his housekeeper and I'm seeing him about it all this morning. It'll be my first job.'

'Well, I'm very pleased for you, Jane, about time you had a bit of happiness. A nice-looking man, that new Rector of ours!' said Mr Peters with a wink. Jane blushed. 'I won't keep you any more; glad of the chance to stop and have a word these days, though, the Missus isn't so good and my rheumatism's getting worse, especially feel it when I'm biking up this hill!'

'Oh, dear, I'm sorry to hear Mrs Peters is not well. I'll come and see her soon – and would you like me to mention it to the Rector?' asked Jane.

'Yes, yes, that would be welcome, Jane, I'd be glad if you would, thank you. Goodbye!' said Mr Peters.

'Goodbye, Mr Peters, and love to Mrs Peters!' said Jane as he rode off on his bicycle waving his hand.

Jane reached the Rectory gateway and her heart started to beat rapidly. She saw Brandy under the pear-tree, full length, soaking up the sun. As she walked along the driveway he opened one eye and Jane giggled. Brandy opened the other eye and raised his ears and, seeing Jane, sprang up and ran barking towards her as though greeting an old friend.

'Hello, Brandy!' she exclaimed as he jumped up her and gave her face a huge lick. 'I hope you've been a good boy!' she said, still giggling. 'I've come to see your master, Brandy, you go and enjoy your snooze,' she teased, and off he went back to his favourite spot under the pear-tree.

Jane used the large brass knocker on the front door, even though she still possessed the key, and soon it opened.

'Jane!' exclaimed Father Stephen. There seemed to be a look of absolute wonder on his face just for a moment.

'Hello, Father, I hope I'm not too late but with one thing and another I was delayed somewhat this morning,' said Jane, feeling that talking would hide her nervousness.

'No, no, not at all, come in,' said Father Stephen, opening the door wider. 'I've been busy trying to replace a washer on a bathroom tap, such a brute it was to screw off, but it's done!' he said. Jane smiled; she was thinking desperately of something to say, but words failed her. Father Stephen led Jane into the study and sat behind his desk, hands clasped in front of him and looking intently at her.

'I meant to ask you last night how your hands were, Jane. I hope they're better,' he said.

'Oh, they're quite healed now, Father,' said Jane, showing him her upturned hands.

'Good, I'm pleased to hear it,' he said. 'Now about the job, Jane,' he said smiling, 'I'm afraid I won't be able to pay you...'

'I'm not looking for payment, Father,' interrupted Jane, 'just some employment. I'm well provided for at the orphanage.'

'But surely you don't want to be there all your life, Jane?' questioned Father Stephen.

'No... of course not, I'd love a home of my own one day, but I don't mind working for nothing. I mean, I'd enjoy coming here and cleaning, and if you wanted me to cook I could do that as well,' said Jane.

'I'd be very pleased for you to cook for me, Jane, but I'm afraid a priest's life is here, there and everywhere, and I'd rarely be able to have set mealtimes.'

'I quite understand, Father,' said Jane, feeling somewhat perturbed at this line of conversation. She felt he was testing her, seeing if she was up to the job. But then she supposed that's what every employer did. 'I could prepare food for you and leave it in the fridge, and then you could have it when you were able to,' said Jane.

'Yes, indeed, that would be a good idea.' He hesitated, then said, 'I hope sometimes, Jane, you would be able to take a meal with me, as a sort of payment, for what you do.'

Jane stared at him and said, 'Well, I suppose I could... I assumed I would be taking all my meals at the orphanage...'

'I'm sure we can sort something out, Jane,' said Father Stephen. 'Could you start today?' he asked.

'Oh, yes, of course, I came prepared with some cleaning materials,' said Jane. 'Do you need any shopping doing while I'm here?'

'I was making a list earlier,' he said. 'Here it is.' He handed her a list of items and she glanced at it.

'I can get most of these from the corner shop, and Mr Stuart, the butcher, has very good cuts of meat, but his prices are not the cheapest,' she informed him.

'I suppose that can't be helped until I can get into town for them, but do you think he might have something cheap for Brandy?' he said, grinning.

'I'm sure he would!' said Jane, and they laughed.

'Well, I'd appreciate it if you could get those things for me,' he said. 'I'll give you some money,' and saying that fished in his trousers pocket for a crumpled ten pound note. 'That should cover it,' he said.

'Thank you,' said Jane. 'Well if there's nothing else, Father, I'll be on my way and start the cleaning when I return. I still have the front door key.'

'That's fine,' he said. 'By the way I may not be in when you get back, I'm going sick visiting and then I've a wedding rehearsal at 2.30 p.m. in church. I'll just have to snatch something to eat in between,' he said, rather ruefully.

'Would you like a ham salad and crusty bread?' said Jane.

'Oh, that sounds wonderful,' sighed Father Stephen, and grinned.

'I'll be going then,' said Jane, rising and walking to the door. 'Oh, I've just remembered, on my way here I met old

Mr Peters. He used to be verger here many years ago and suffers with rheumatism, and his wife has cancer, so I did tell him I'd mention their names to you; they would like it if you visited them.'

'I'll put them down on my list,' said Father Stephen reaching for a notepad. 'What's their address?'

'It's Rose Cottage, Mill Lane. None of the houses in Mill Lane have numbers,' Jane informed him.

'I'll see them later today, Jane, thank you.'

As they walked through the hall to the front door Jane asked, 'I suppose it's Lucy Richards' wedding rehearsal?'

'Yes, it is,' said Father Stephen. 'Do you know her?'

'Oh, yes, we used to play together as children and then she went to the Grammar School in town and we lost touch,' explained Jane.

'I suppose you know nearly everyone in the village, Jane!' said Father Stephen.

'Nearly everyone! Except for those coming to live in the new housing estate on The Meadows. They seem to keep themselves to themselves and rarely come into the village centre to shop,' said Jane.

'Modern life, Jane!' exclaimed Father Stephen. 'They want to have a quiet life living in a village and yet they have cars and are never in the place. Most of them are commuting to London or elsewhere and sending their children to the schools in town and shopping outside the village too! We shall probably only see them in church for baptisms, weddings and funerals,' he said rather grimly.

'The church should not be used like that!' said Jane, vehemently.

'Quite right, Jane, I totally agree with you, but that's the way things are these days. One must try to encourage them when they do come, so that the Church has a future. By the way, is there a Sunday School here? I meant to ask Mr Scott.'

'Yes, there is, Father, quite a healthy one,' said Jane. 'In fact I'm one of the teachers!'

'Good!' said Father Stephen, 'I'm pleased to hear it,' he said as they walked together through the front door and down the drive. Brandy came bounding up to them, barking. 'We've been neglecting you, Brandy, that won't do!' said Father Stephen, laughing.

'May I take him shopping with me, Father?'

'Of course! He's not had much exercise today, I'll get his lead.' While Father Stephen went back into the Rectory Jane stroked Brandy and talked to him.

'I'll take you up onto the heath sometimes, Brandy, you'll like it there. Lots of rabbits to run after!'

'Here it is, Jane,' said Father Stephen. 'See you later!'

'Thank you, Father, see you later!' she said.

Chapter Three

Saturday dawned and Lucy Richards' wedding was the talk of the village. She was to marry Nick Johnson, the eldest son of a wealthy bank manager in London. By the look of the flowers in church, and the gleaming white Bentley outside their home, no expense had been spared! Jane had not been to the Rectory that morning as there was nothing to be done and the pantry was well stocked and besides Matron needed her to run some errands. Jane felt happy these days, she had no nightmares about her parents' death and hoped she had put all that behind her. She did intend to go to the church for the wedding, partly to see Lucy and partly to see how Father Stephen conducted his first wedding in the village, so she set off for the church.

She waited at the lychgate while the photographer performed his duties with the bridesmaids and then slipped into church and sat at the back. There was no sign of Father Stephen, but then she saw him walking up the north aisle from the vestry, wearing a white cope and stole. She thought he looked so... handsome! She shut her eyes and bowed her head.

'Oh, dear God,' she said to herself, 'I mustn't think of him like that, please help me!'

She heard a rustle behind her and looking round momentarily saw Father Stephen smiling down at her. She smiled briefly and then closed her eyes again in torment.

When she opened them she saw him at the porch door talking to Lucy. She wished she hadn't come to the church. Why did she feel like this? The Bridal March began and everyone stood up. Father Stephen led the way down the aisle, smiling. Lucy looked very beautiful in her brilliant white dress with red roses in her hair and bouquet. She had a Matron of Honour and two small bridesmaids in crimson dresses with white roses – a stark contrast to the bride.

The service progressed but Jane seemed to be in a world of her own. She heard odd snatches of the vows and sang the hymns, but felt oppressed by the crowd in front of her. As soon as the Wedding March started she slipped out of church and ran as fast as she could to the heath until she could run no more and, collapsing on the ground, began to sob uncontrollably. 'Oh, why do I feel like this?' she gasped. Then she suddenly knew. She loved Father Stephen but as he was a celibate she couldn't express her feelings. Then why did he pay her so much attention? Could he possibly love her? It would be wrong for him to do so. She felt so confused. 'Oh, dear Lord, please help me!' she pleaded. She heard a voice saying, 'Calm yourself, Jane, everything will be all right.' She thought it sounded like her father's voice; she looked around her but saw no one, only a yellowhammer singing on the top of a gorse bush and the heather swaying gently in the warm breeze. She sat quietly for a few minutes listening to the birds and the gently running stream a few feet away from her. She felt calm, as though a weight had been lifted from her shoulders. 'Thank you, God,' she said simply. 'I do feel better now.'

She went back to the orphanage. She wondered if she should ever go to the Rectory again. 'Please tell me what I'm to do, Lord,' she asked. She began to feel sick with worry. 'I want to go, and yet I don't!' she said to herself. Matron met her on the stairs.

'Is there anything wrong, Jane?' she asked, sounding very concerned. 'You don't look at all well, dear.'

'I... just feel a little under the weather. I'll go to my room,' she said.

'Have a lie down for a while,' advised Matron. 'You've been doing so much lately, it's catching up with you.'

'Yes, you're probably right,' said Jane, not wanting to be drawn into any more conversation.

On reaching her bedroom Jane washed her face and lay down on the bed closing her eyes and before long she was sound asleep. A cool waft of air from the half open window woke her and she noticed the setting sun just going behind a distant hill. 'I must have slept for ages!' she said reaching out for her bedside clock. 'Four hours!' There was a gentle knock at the door and Matron entered.

'Hello, Jane!' she said, sitting on the side of the bed. 'I came up an hour ago but you were fast asleep. I hope you're feeling better.'

'Yes, thank you, Matron, much better,' said Jane.

'The Rector rang,' said Matron.

'Oh, did he,' said Jane, trying not to sound interested.

'Yes, about five o'clock,' she said. 'He appeared to be expecting you to go for tea, but I told him you weren't well and had gone to bed.'

'Oh, dear, I quite forgot!' said Jane.

'Never mind, dear, I said you should be well enough to be at church tomorrow so you can sort something out then,' said Matron, rising to leave. 'Would you like something to eat now? I can bring you a tray.'

'No thank you,' said Jane. Matron opened the door and Jane said, 'Matron!'

'Yes, Jane.'

'I... Oh, nothing, thank you,' stammered Jane.

'I'll leave you to get a little more rest, then,' said Matron, closing the door.

Jane had a shower, put on her dressing-gown and went into the library for a book. She felt quite awake now and wanted to read quietly so she took the book back to her room. Anything to get her mind off Father Stephen, she thought. Tomorrow would come soon enough. 'Please help me, God, please!' she muttered.

Chapter Four

The sermon had been a short one and not up to his usual high standard. Father Stephen had conducted the service in a subdued voice, at least that was how Jane thought of it. There's something wrong! thought Jane. Oh, dear Lord, I don't want him to be unhappy. I hope its not my fault! The last hymn ended and the congregation began to make their way slowly to the south door where Father Stephen shook their hands mechanically and wished them all good morning. And now it was Jane's turn. She was nearly last.

'Jane!' he said, taking her hand and holding it tightly. 'Are you all right?' His expression was one of great concern. 'I thought we were going to have tea together yesterday,' he said.

'Yes, I... sorry, I forgot... I didn't feel too well, but I'm fine now. How are you?' she asked.

'I've been worried about you...' he said, being interrupted by a young couple wanting to ask him about a wedding date. 'See you tomorrow, Jane,' he said anxiously, still holding her hand. 'You will be there?' he asked.

'Yes, I'll be there,' said Jane, smiling. He returned her smile and was gone. 'Thank you for helping me, Father,' she said in prayer as she left the church. Jane felt she had found renewed strength. I've got to help him, she thought. It's a demanding parish and he needs help. I must be strong for him. Please give me strength to cope, Lord. I know I can do it!

The following day Jane went to the Rectory and found Brandy, as usual, under the pear-tree. He greeted her with so much fervour that he nearly knocked her down. He wouldn't stop barking, and Father Stephen, wondering what the noise was about, came to the front door and began laughing.

'He's missed you, Jane!' he said, as she approached him with Brandy still jumping around her. 'We both have!' Changing the subject he said, 'I've a funeral at the crematorium at eleven thirty, Jane, but don't worry if there are any phone calls, I'll put the answerphone on. Oh, and there are one or two items I need from the grocer's, if you wouldn't mind, please.'

'Of course not, Father,' she said. 'I've a letter to post and one or two other errands as well. Do you know when you'll be back?'

'Could be around one o'clock because I need to do some business in town,' he replied. 'You will be here when I get back?' he asked. 'I'm free most of the afternoon until the church meeting tonight,' he informed. 'We could have lunch together.'

'I'll see to it,' she said smiling. She thought he seemed much calmer today. She felt so relieved. The telephone rang.

'I'll get it,' he said. 'Then I must go.'

Jane fetched Brandy's lead and off they went to the shops, Jane posting her letter on the way. The village was quiet this morning and she finished her shopping quickly so she decided to take Brandy for a run on the heath. She felt so contented, quite the reverse to Saturday. She sat down by the stream dangling her hand in the cool water.

She could see Brandy on the other side and he swam across to her. As he shook himself Jane became rather wet.

'Oh, Brandy!' she exclaimed, 'I've already had one shower this morning!'

'Woof!' he replied, and lay down beside her, his head on her lap. She stroked him for a while and looked around her. There was hardly a cloud in the sky. She loved this place and never wanted to leave it. She sighed.

'Time to go, Brandy,' she said, 'jobs to do for your master.'

By the time they got back to the Rectory it was nearly noon. Jane prepared a casserole and a lemon meringue pie while Brandy went into the back garden gnawing at a large bone the butcher had let her have.

She heard footsteps in the hall. 'I'm home, Jane!' came Father Stephen's voice.

'I'm in the kitchen, Father,' shouted Jane.

As he entered he said, 'That smells good, Jane. I wish I had time to prepare such a meal, but it tastes better when it's prepared by someone else!' he grinned.

'Flattery will get you nowhere, Father!' said Jane, reciprocating his grin.

'Oh, what a shame,' he said, teasing her.

Jane said, 'There's some post for you. I've put it in the study.'

'Thank you, I'll see to it now,' he said.

There were three items, one from a charity; a long form to fill in for the diocese, at which he groaned, and a letter reminding him of an annual clergy conference in London the following month which would last four days! He knew he had to go, so that meant getting relief for his weekday services and arranging cover for any funerals which may arise during his absence. He looked in his organiser and picking up the telephone dialled a local number. He was very thankful to have a retired priest living in the village, now fast becoming a suburb. He was engaged with the call for about fifteen minutes. He enjoyed talking to Father Gerald and had on more than one occasion, during his first few days in the parish, consulted him on numerous matters.

'That's one job out of the way,' he said to himself as he put down the receiver. There was a knock at the door and Jane entered.

'Luncheon is served!' she said in a grand manner. Father Stephen laughed.

'And I'm ready for it!' he replied.

Chapter Five

As the weeks progressed Father Stephen seemed to be settling in very well. He appeared happy and worked well with his congregation. They arranged fund-raising events and other social functions and collections almost doubled. For once in many years they were able to pay their quota.

There had been a spate of weddings and this Saturday was no exception. Jane usually went and sat at the back of the church as she did the first time he took one. She loved to see the professionally arranged flowers and the beautiful wedding dresses. She left the orphanage early and on her way called in to see Mr and Mrs Peters. Mrs Peters' condition was worsening and the doctor had only given her a few months to live. They had a nurse in daily to wash and dress her but Mr Peters had to do everything else, so Jane went to relieve him of this task. When she arrived he was feeding his wife with rice pudding.

'I'll do that, Mr Peters,' said Jane. 'I noticed the garden centre had just received a fresh supply of bedding plants, and I know how much you like them, I'll stay here with Mrs Peters until you get back.'

'Thank you, Jane,' said Mr Peters, looking rather tired. 'I meant to go and have a look-see when they arrived. I'll walk down, my rheumatism is playing me up something chronic today,' he said rubbing his hip. 'I won't be long.'

Jane finished feeding Mrs Peters, who seemed to be having difficulty swallowing. She then made her a cup of tea and settled down to read to her for a while, keeping a watchful eye on the clock. It was one o'clock and the wedding was in an hour's time.

Just as Mr Peters arrived home, his wife began coughing up blood. Jane was very concerned and Mr Peters was near panic.

'We must ring Doctor Andrews, Mr Peters!' said Jane, rather anxiously. Mr Peters cradled his wife's head in his arms and looked up at Jane,

'Would you do it please, Jane,' he said, looking very frightened.

'Yes, of course,' she said, running to the telephone in the hall. The number was in the address book on the hall table. Jane finally received an answer and was relieved to hear Doctor Andrews' voice. She told him the problem and he said he would be around within a quarter of an hour. Jane went back into the living room and Mrs Peters was now having difficulty breathing. Within ten minutes Doctor Andrews arrived and immediately rang for an ambulance. Mr Peters went to put on his coat and Jane asked,

'Is there anything I can do, Mr Peters?'

'I don't think so, Jane,' he said with tears in his eyes. 'I don't think it will be long now. Thank you for all you've done, Jane, it's very much appreciated.'

'Not at all, Mr Peters,' said Jane, feeling she would soon start crying.

The ambulance arrived and soon rushed Mrs Peters to the nearby hospital. The time was two twenty. The wedding would be nearly over. She decided to go straight to the Rectory to prepare Father Stephen's tea. She felt so tired and said a prayer for Mrs Peters. She had known for a long time that she was dying, but is anyone really ready for it when it does come? Brandy greeted her with his usual welcome of wagging tail and jumping around her and this brightened her a little.

She went into the kitchen and decided to make a bread-and-butter pudding preceded by a salmon salad. She heard the front door bang and went into the hall saying that she had made his favourite pudding but she was not prepared for what she saw. Father Stephen glared at her, breathing heavily, then he said in a very gruff voice, 'You were not at the wedding!'

Jane was absolutely dumbstruck. 'I... called on Mr and Mrs Peters on my way to church...' she said stammering, so horrified at his temper. 'Mrs Peters had to be rushed into hospital.' Just as she said the last word he strode towards the open study door and slammed it shut behind him. Brandy started whining and pawing at door. Jane tried to pull him away by his collar. 'No, Brandy,' she said quietly, 'he doesn't want us. Come away.' Brandy went with her reluctantly to the kitchen where she turned off the oven as the pudding was done. Then she took Brandy, still holding on to his collar, out to the heath for a walk.

Meanwhile Father Stephen sat at his desk, his head in his hands. 'Oh dear, God, why was I angry with her for not being there?' He was breathing nervously and felt unable to control himself. The telephone rang and he stared at it, terrified. He quickly turned on the answerphone and shut his eyes. 'I must go and apologise to her,' he said to himself. He breathed deeply to try to hide his nervousness and went into the kitchen. She wasn't there, neither was Brandy. He called her name but there was no reply. 'She must have taken Brandy for a walk,' he murmured.

Back in the study he looked down at the sheet of paper in front of him, devoid of words, for tomorrow's sermon. He couldn't remember which text he was going to use. He looked at the gospel reading for the day and began to write. Page after page he screwed up and threw into the wastepaper basket. It was no good, he couldn't concentrate! He needed Jane. How long would she be? He started to breathe nervously again and poured a two-finger measure of whisky from the table near the window. He sat down again, closed his eyes and being very exhausted soon fell asleep.

By this time Jane and Brandy had reached the heath by the narrow lane which ran through it. Both of them were very subdued and Brandy kept whining. 'He wants to be on his own, Brandy,' she said. 'He's in a bad mood.' They took one of the numerous paths to the left of the lane walking through the purple heather and yellow gorse. Brandy soon began sniffing around and ran off chasing a rabbit. Jane sauntered on, her head down. The quietness on the heath was suddenly broken by a screech of brakes and a thud. Jane looked around her and saw a van in the lane, the driver was just getting out. For a moment the scene didn't register and then she called Brandy's name. She ran towards the van, still calling, and by now knowing what awful tragedy had occurred. The man was crouching in front of the van and she could see Brandy's motionless body. She knelt down and stroked his head.

'Brandy,' she cried. 'Oh, Brandy, no!'

'I'm sorry, Miss,' said the van driver, wringing his cap in his hands, 'he ran straight in front of me. I swerved but I couldn't miss him. I'll take him back home for you, Miss. Where do you live?'

Jane stared at him, tears running down her face, hardly believing that Brandy was dead. 'The Rectory,' she said, hardly audibly.

The van driver, whose name was Bob, lifted Brandy's body with difficulty into the back of the van and told Jane to get in. In silence they made their way back to the Rectory and Bob drove through the gates. Jane rushed out and ran into the house and without knocking burst into the study. Father Stephen looked up in surprise, and seeing Jane's tear-stained face said, 'Jane, what's wrong?'

'Brandy's dead!' Jane blurted out.

'Brandy!' said Father Stephen, incredulously, 'dead!'

'It's all my fault!' said Jane, 'I didn't take his lead. We went to the heath and he chased a rabbit and a van knocked him down.' By now she was sobbing and could hardly speak. 'The van driver has brought him back,' she added.

Father Stephen looked out of the window and saw the van with the rear doors open and Bob wringing his cap in his hands looking very forlorn. He turned back to Jane. He desperately wanted to comfort her; to put his arms round her, but restrained himself and said quietly, 'I'll go and see.'

Jane watched him go, tears streaming down her face. She saw him walk to the back of the van and talk to Bob and then look inside. The two men lifted Brandy's body out and put it at the side of the drive near the pear-tree. A few more words were exchanged, then Bob got into the van and reversed out of the drive. When he had gone Jane went outside and stood beside Father Stephen, looking down at Brandy.

'I'll fetch a spade and bury him under the pear-tree,' said Father Stephen, rolling up his shirtsleeves and going to the shed. Jane knelt down and took off Brandy's collar. She wanted to keep it. She stroked his head again and said, 'I'm sorry, Brandy!'

Father Stephen came back and began digging. 'Is there anything I can do?' asked Jane.

He looked at her and smiled, 'A nice cup of tea wouldn't come amiss, Jane.'

'Okay, I'll put the kettle on,' she said, taking one last look at the dog. As she went inside she thought how changed Father Stephen was. So calm. And yet earlier he could hardly contain his anger. She set up a tray with a teapot and two cups, sugar bowl and milk jug and took it into the study. By this time Father Stephen had finished and was sitting at his desk. As Jane approached him he stood up and took the tray off her, putting it down on a nearby table. He could see she was still very distressed. He put his hands on her shoulders and said, 'Jane, I'm sorry!' She put her arms round him and with her head on his shoulder began sobbing. He felt a great sense of calm. She wanted him to comfort her and that, he thought, was half the battle over.

'It's all my fault,' she said between sobs.

'No, Jane,' he said quietly, stroking her hair, 'it's my fault entirely. I shouldn't have been angry earlier. You wouldn't have taken him for a walk if I hadn't. I was so used to seeing you at the weddings, I... just expected you to be there,' he said. She looked up at him, red-eyed and bewildered. She couldn't understand why it was so important to him that she should be there. 'Let's have that cup of tea,' he said, releasing her. He felt that if he held her much longer he might kiss her and it would not be the right moment.

'I'll be going now,' said Jane, abruptly putting down her cup.

'I'll drive you back,' said Father Stephen rising with her.

'No... please, I'd rather walk, thank you,' stammered Jane.

Father Stephen was about to protest but thought the better of it. 'All right, Jane,' he said, 'don't worry about the tray, I'll see to it.'

'Goodbye,' said Jane.

'Goodbye, Jane, see you tomorrow.'

She looked at him mournfully and made no reply. He watched her through the window walking down the drive. She stopped at the mound of newly dug earth under the pear-tree and wiped her eyes. Then she had gone through the Rectory gates and he could no longer see her because of the high hedge. Father Stephen picked up the telephone and dialled the orphanage number. He got through to the Matron straight away and told her what had happened. At least she would be able to comfort Jane on her return. He then drew some sheets of blank paper towards him and wrote the text for his sermon 'St John's Gospel, chapter 15 verse 13: Greater love, hath no man than this; that a man lay down his life for his friends.' He felt that Brandy's death had brought them together in love. Page after page he wrote, the words flowing from him as they had never done before. He read it through and was astonished at how well it sounded. He hoped his congregation would think so.

Jane hardly noticed anything on her slow walk back to the orphanage. She barely had the energy to lift her head to the bright sunshine and warm breeze. She didn't see or hear the twittering birds in the hedges or the scurrying squirrels. She climbed the hill and felt exhausted. Matron was waiting for her at the door. 'Come along, Jane,' she said, putting an arm round her shoulders. 'Father Stephen rang and told me all about what happened; he's very concerned about you,' she added.

'Is he?' is all Jane could say. They went into Matron's office and had a chat and Jane began to feel better. She went to her room and changed, washed her face and helped cook with the tea.

That night she lay awake thinking about Father Stephen. He had comforted her and she had felt so thankful for it, but what had she done for him? He must feel dreadful. After all, Brandy was his dog. She wanted to talk to him; to give him some words of comfort, but of course it was too late in the evening to do so. She hoped she would have a chance to speak to him after service tomorrow morning.

Chapter Six

As he had hoped, his sermon was a great success and everyone made some comment to him after the service. They also told him how saddened they were to bear of Brandy's death and tried to make light of it by saying that his next dog must be called Rum!

Father Stephen was anxious to talk to Jane and at last was able to. 'Jane,' he said, 'that conference starts tomorrow in London; I think in the circumstances I'll not go.' He did not tell her he did not want to leave her at such a time.

'But you must go, Father!' she encouraged. 'It will take your mind off things. You really must.'

'Okay,' he said, rather reluctantly, 'I suppose you're right,' and gave her a smile. 'Are you all right, Jane?' he added.

'Yes, I'm okay,' she said quietly and smiled up at him. 'Are you?' she asked.

'Yes, I'm fine,' he said, not really feeling as fine as he sounded. 'I'll be back Thursday evening, Jane,' he said in the hope that she might be there.

'See you then,' she said.

He held out his hand to her and she took it firmly. 'See you, Jane,' he said.

'Goodbye, Father,' Jane replied.

The following day Father Stephen set off early for London. He had a two-hour drive ahead of him. The first item on the agenda was an introduction by the President followed by a short meeting, then lunch, then another meeting. Father Stephen met some of his theological college friends and they reminisced on old times. It was not until the second day that he began to feel homesick. He kept thinking of Jane and wondering what she would be doing while he was away. Would she even go to the Rectory?

At breakfast on the last day he was sitting with a couple of old friends and as was unusual for him he was rather quiet. 'There's something on your mind, Stephen,' said Father Michael, 'want to talk about it?'

'Oh, I'm sorry, Michael,' said Father Stephen, apologising, 'I'm afraid I was miles away,' which was absolutely right. In his mind he was with Jane. He wanted to get back to her. 'Michael,' he said, 'I must get back. Would you make my apologies for the final meeting, please?' he said rising.

'Of course, Stephen,' said Father Michael, 'and if there's anything I can do, you know where I am.'

'Yes, Michael,' he said, 'thanks. I'll be in touch. Goodbye.'

'Goodbye, Stephen,' said Father Michael. 'Take care!'

Father Stephen rushed to his room to pack his belongings and sprinted to his car. He had to get back. He needed to see Jane. 'Oh, please, God,' he said quietly, 'let her be there. She must be there!' He almost reached a panic state and tried to calm himself 'Slow down, you idiot,' he kept saying. 'She must be there.'

He reached the country lanes of his own county and rounded a bend. He had to break hard as a farmer was herding a flock of sheep along the road into a field. He gripped the wheel and wanted to shout to them to get out of the way. Eventually there was room to pass and he put his foot down again. He was breathing heavily and could feel the panic rising up in him. 'Oh, please, God,' he said again, 'let her be at the Rectory when I get there, please!'

Only two more miles now and he had made the journey in an hour and a half. He drove through the Rectory gates and came to an abrupt halt. He got out of the car and ran to the front door fumbling with his key. 'Calm yourself!' he muttered. He went into the hall and shutting the door behind him leaned on it for a few moments, closing his eyes. 'Jane,' he shouted, but there was no reply. He shouted even louder 'Jane! I'm home.' He looked round the hall in desperation and then he heard a noise from above. He looked up the stairway and Jane appeared on the landing holding a duster.

'Father,' she cried, 'you're back early!'

The joy on her face at seeing him filled him with so much happiness that he felt his heart would burst. She ran down the stairs and into his open arms. 'I've missed you terribly!' she said, clinging to him.

'I couldn't be away from you a moment longer, Jane,' he said holding her tightly. 'Jane,' he said softly.

'Yes,' said Jane looking up at him.

'I love you,' he said looking straight into her eyes.

'I love you, Stephen,' she said, using his Christian name for the first time.

'The first day I saw you digging in the garden I knew I loved you but I went away trying to forget you but I couldn't. I had to come back.' Before she could say anything he said, 'Will you marry me?' almost holding his breath.

'Yes, darling,' she said, 'I'll marry you.' It was then that he kissed her and Jane thought how gentle he was.

'How soon can we be married, Stephen?' asked Jane, her head on his shoulder.

'I'll start the banns this Sunday, Jane,' he said, kissing her forehead. 'There's nothing we have to wait for.'

'Can I tell Matron?' asked Jane 'She's been like a mother to me.'

'Okay,' said Stephen and smiled, 'but only Matron! I'd like to see the faces of those in church on Sunday when they hear the banns. It'll be such a surprise to them.'

'Stephen,' said Jane, rather shyly.

'Yes, dear,' replied Stephen.

'I haven't any money,' said Jane apologetically.

'Dear Jane,' said Stephen, 'we have each other and a roof over our heads, what more do we want?'

'Well,' said Jane, stroking the curls of hair in his neck, 'some children.'

'Some children!' said Stephen, trying to look astonished, 'How many?'

'How many would you like, darling?' said Jane.

'Let's talk about that after we're married,' said Stephen, and grinned mischievously.

Sunday dawned and Father Stephen awoke feeling very nervous. He felt it only etiquette to tell his wardens of his impending marriage before reading the banns and they were absolutely thrilled, telling him that the parish needed a dedicated couple and that no one could be more suited than he and Jane. They were particularly pleased for Jane as she had had such an unhappy early life.

The service proceeded as usual up until the time when the banns were to be read. Father Stephen stood up and said, 'I publish the banns of marriage between,' and then paused for a slight moment, his heart beating rapidly 'Stephen James, bachelor of this parish, and Jane West, spinster of this parish. This is for the first time of asking,' and before he could ask if there were any just cause or impediment why they should not be joined together, the congregation burst into a round of applause and cheers. Tears came to his eyes and he looked at Jane, sitting in the front pew. She was smiling bravely at him and he could see a tear fall onto her cheek. He went to her, and pulling her to her feet turned her round to stand with him. The cheering eventually subsided and he finished what he was reading, then said, 'Jane and I would like to thank you all very much for such a marvellous response to our good news. We know we shall be very happy together and are very grateful for your support. Thank you.'

'Thank you,' said Jane.

Another round of applause and Jane returned to her seat and the service continued with the blessing and the final hymn.

After the service both Jane and Father Stephen stood at the door to shake hands with everyone. The pleasure on the faces of each and every member of the congregation was overwhelming. Matron stood with a handkerchief to her eyes wishing them every happiness.

When they were alone Father Stephen turned to Jane and taking her in his arms, he kissed her

'Really, Father!' she teased, 'in church!'

'Wait till I get home, Jane,' he said with an impish grin.

'Yes,' she breathed, 'home!'

With that Father Stephen went into the vestry singing the hymn, 'O perfect love, all human thought transcending', while Jane stepped out into the bright autumn sunshine, extremely happy for the first time in her life.